# WESTWARD HO WITH OLLIE OX!

**MELANIE RICHARDSON DUNDY**
Cover design by David J. Kelliher

MDCT MDCT Publishing, South Beach, Oregon

ISBN  0-9674491-4-6

Library of Congress Catalog Card Number:  99-96010

MDCT Publishing
5946 SW Cupola Drive
South Beach, OR   97366

541.867.4215
ollieox@teleport.com

For Mike, David, Karel and Sandy -


the four people who never stopped
believing in me
and never let me stop believing in myself.

# I am an ox.
# Ollie Ox to be more precise.

Oh, I know I'm cute
(some have even said handsome),
but I weigh almost 2000 pounds so I guess
I'm not very cuddly.

I live with the
Tylers on a farm.  I
sleep in the barn.

They won't let me in their house.  That's because I am too
big - **much too big** - to walk through the front door.  The
whole house would probably come
crashing down on me if I tried.

I am dependable, though, and I am very proud.
Don't I look proud in my picture?
These traits along with my size and my tremendous
strength are what led the Tylers to choose me for
the very long journey they took in the year 1844.

I am not one to boast but,
if the truth be told,
I, Ollie, an ox born of humble roots,
am the STAR of this story.

Let me tell you all about it . . . . . .

As I've already mentioned, I belong to the Tyler family;
Mr. Tyler, Mrs. Tyler and their son, Johnny.
Maybe you will come back and draw a picture of my
family after you learn more about them.

OOPS!  I almost forgot to mention a very important member
of our family -
RORY!

One evening, after working all day in the fields of our farm, Mr. Tyler made an announcement to his family:

"We are going to Oregon in a covered wagon!  We will go by way of the Oregon Trail.  It will be a new chance for us; a chance for wealth and adventure!"

Johnny stared down at his shoes
and thought about that for awhile.
He had never heard the word *Oregon* before so he had no idea what his father was talking about.
Johnny knew better than to question
his father's decision, though.

The Tylers lived in Independence, Missouri,
and Mr. Tyler was going to move them all to Oregon.

Can you find Independence, Missouri on this map of
the United States?

(Hint:  Independence, Missouri)

Can you find Oregon
and the end of the
Oregon Trail on the map
of the United States?

(Hint: The end of the trail in Oregon)

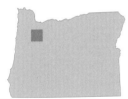

Now draw a line between Missouri and Oregon.

It's a long way, isn't it?
It's actually about 2000 miles and would take the Tylers
about 6 months to make the trip.

(Do you live anywhere near Independence, Missouri?
Can you find your home on the map?)

1.) Do you know how long it would take you to fly
(in an airplane)
from Independence, Missouri
to Portland, Oregon?

write down that time below.

2.) Now see if you can figure out how
long it would take you to drive
the same distance
(that is if you had your driver's license).

Now write that time below.

**Trip to Oregon**

Time it would take the Tylers to travel to Oregon:      _____6 months_____

Time it would take you to fly from Missouri to Oregon:      _____

Time it would take you to drive from Missouri to Oregon:      _____

*WOW, you would be able to get there a lot faster than the Tylers did!!!!!!!!!!*

In making the decision to travel west in 1844,
the Tylers became members of
a very special group of emigrants who would become
known as pioneers once they settled in Oregon.


Let me, Ollie Ox,
tell you about these emigrants.

They were brave people who left their homes to travel west
across America to states such as Oregon and California.
They had to leave behind friends and family members
knowing they might never see them again.


Do you think you could be that brave?

Think how hard it would be for you to leave all your friends.  Johnny was very, very sad about leaving his best friend, Will.

Do you have a best friend with whom you share all your secrets?
Can you imagine how hard it would be to say good-bye knowing you probably would never see or talk to that friend again?

Johnny cried and cried before we left.  Oh, he was looking forward to the adventure he and his family were about to have, but he wanted his friends to be able to share that adventure.

What he didn't know was that he would make new friends on the journey.

Johnny felt better when he
realized that he would be
able to take along his true
and loyal friend,


RORY.

Many of the pioneer families took their pets
with them.

Can you draw a picture of either your pet or an
imaginary pet that you would have wanted to take
along to keep you company on your journey west?

The Tylers purchased a covered wagon
in which to travel.

It looked like this.

When the pioneer
families going on the
journey lined up all
their wagons behind
one another, they
formed a *wagon train.*

It was a traveling community.

Can you see why they called it a wagon TRAIN?

At first, the wagon looked really, really big, but
then they all climbed inside to try it out –
first Johnny,
then Mrs. Tyler and then Mr. Tyler.

And last, but definitely not least, RORY.

All of a sudden, the wagon
didn't seem quite so big.

Where were they going to put all the things
they would need for the trip?
And what about their treasures?
I knew Mrs. Tyler would never leave behind the
beautiful quilt her friends had made for her
to take on the journey. The quilt would be a
wonderful memory of home especially since
Mrs. Tyler's friends had embroidered their names on it.

I, of course, would take up no room in the wagon
because a big ox like me would be hitched
to the *outside* of the wagon.

Mrs. Tyler decided the solution to the problem of space was
ORGANIZATION!

That's what it would take!!

And they would each have to do his or her part.
That was all there was to it!!

(Poor Johnny had a hard time organizing his stuff in his own bedroom.  He really wanted to do his part, but he had absolutely no idea where to start or what to do to load ALL his family's belongings into only one wagon.)

Mr. Tyler and Mrs. Tyler decided to make extra room in the wagon by hanging as much as they possibly could on the outside and underneath of the wagon.

Here are just some of the things they planned to carry on the outside of the wagon. How do you think each was to be used?

(When you think about the use for this pail, think of Jesse, our cow)

(Hint: Mrs. Tyler sewed linen sacks which she filled with salt, sugar and flour to make bread. Although the Tyler's basic diet would consist of bread and bacon, Mrs. Tyler also packed rice, chipped beef, dried beans and dried fruit in barrels which would be used to store water when they were empty of food. These foods would not provide much variety, but they would provide nourishment.)

How do you think you would have done on such a diet?  Do you think you would have gotten bored eating the same foods every day?

Can you draw pictures of your three absolutely favorite foods in the whole world?

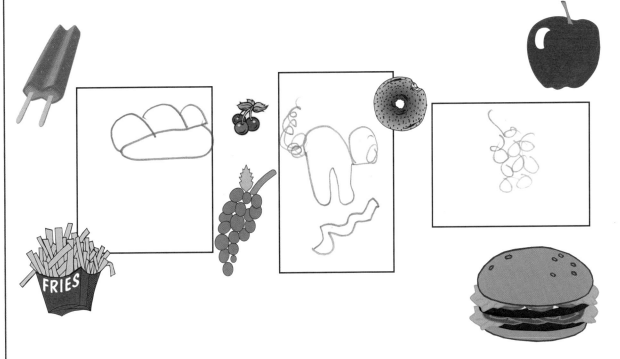

Did these foods exist in 1844?

(Did you draw a picture of hay?
I bet Ollie Ox would have.)

Johnny was told by his parents that, in addition to his clothes, he could bring 5 of his favorite belongings - as long as they were small.

Which of your belongings
would you have chosen to take?

1._____

2._____

3._____

4._____

5._____

It would be hard to leave everything else behind, wouldn't it?

RORY had only
one treasure
that he wanted
to bring

I was lucky because my best friend Herb, who was an ox like me, was also coming on the trip.

I knew I wouldn't get lonely as long as Herb was with me.

Herb and I had the job of pulling my family's
wagon.  So you see how important our job was!
Herb was as strong as
I was so we worked well together.
(He was nowhere near as lovable as me, though.)
We were hooked up to the wagon by a *yoke*.

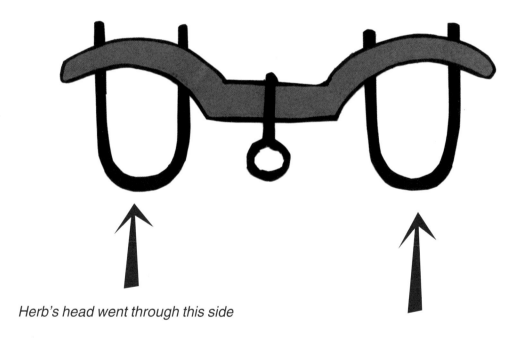

Herb's head went through this side

And mine went through this side

(It doesn't look anything like
the yolk of an egg does it?)

I worked very hard for my family because I knew they were depending on me.  Everyday from sunrise to sunset, Herb and I pulled their wagon.

Of course, I worked the hardest of all the animals on the wagon train!  Well, I did!

I know it isn't polite to brag, but the question is:  Is it bragging when I am merely speaking the truth?!

We pulled the wagon across
creeks and streams and rivers.
It was difficult to pull the
heavy wagon over the rocks

and mud, but the cool water felt good on my tired
legs.  Herb didn't like the cold water or the mud.
He grumbled a lot!  (But then, it was his nature to
grumble a lot!  I was used to it.)

We pulled that wagon over mountains. We pulled it up and up the steep trails until Herb and I thought our backs would break.

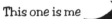
This one is me

We pulled it through valleys. We were able to travel much faster in the valleys than over hills or mountains.

Sometimes we had to cross rivers that were very
deep and filled with dangerous rapids. When Mr. Tyler
knew it would be difficult for Herb and me to pull the
wagon across the water safely, he helped us. He and
three other men from the wagon train guided us by riding
at our sides. Those men held on to our yoke with all their
strength to avoid being swept away by the currents.
There were a few times when, even as big as
I was, I almost lost my footing in the rush of water.
It was frightening but Herb and I persevered.

Johnny rode inside the wagon with RORY. Once when we
were crossing a river, I noticed that Johnny had his
eyes closed and was gripping the side
of the wagon so tightly that his knuckles turned white.
I knew he couldn't swim so I knew he was terrified
the wagon would tip over. I was being very careful and
was determined to keep that wagon
as steady as I possibly could!

I hope that if you're planning to travel with a wagon train,
you will learn to swim first!

Herb and I pulled the wagon
when it poured down rain

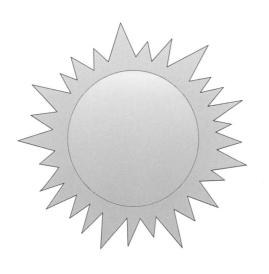

and when it was so hot I thought my head would explode. Herb got really cranky when the weather was hot. He didn't take pride in his work like I did. In fact, you could say that sometimes he was lazy (although I'd never have the nerve to tell him I thought that).

All Herb wanted was to go back home to Missouri where he could sit in the shade of a tree and swat flies with his tail.

When crossing the prairie, it got so dusty that Herb and I had a hard time seeing and breathing. Since Mr. Tyler was a very kind man, he often wiped off our noses and our eyes with a wet cloth to make us more comfortable. Sometimes the wagons rode side by side on the prairies

rather than in a line. That way the families and animals didn't have to breathe quite so much dust.

Even so, Johnny was covered in dirt
as was everything in our wagon.

But we trudged on.

I never complained
(which is more than I can say for Herb).

I knew it was my job to get my family to Oregon.
I just wished someone would tell me where Oregon was
and how long it would take us to get there.
Don't forget, being an ox, I couldn't read a map.

It seemed to be taking forever.

My feet and legs were
really starting to hurt.
Okay so every now and
then I did complain -
but just a little and I
did it quietly.

While crossing the plains, we saw our first Indian. (In years to come, Indians would be known as Native Americans, but they were referred to as Indians when I crossed the plains with my family.) He was standing on the back of his horse watching our wagons pass. The grass was so high that if he had been sitting down on his horse, we couldn't have seen him and he couldn't have seen us.

Can you draw a picture of
the Indian standing on his horse?

Each night the families circled the wagons. They put all the animals in the middle to keep them from running away. Circling the wagons also provided safety and shelter from the winds.

One night when all the families had set up camp, some Indians did approach us, but they were not quite what Johnny had expected. He thought that if he ever saw Indians on the trail, the Indians' faces would be covered with war paint and they would come into camp whooping and hollering and shooting everyone in sight with bows and arrows.

Much to Johnny's surprise, these Indians did not wear war paint.  Oh, they carried bows and arrows but they carried them to hunt food –
not people.

What animals do you think the Indians would have hunted to provide food for their families?

The Indians believed they were one with the land and, therefore, took from the land only what they needed to survive.  That's a good lesson for all of us to learn.

The two Indian men and one Indian boy about Johnny's age who visited our camp gave Johnny and the other children beautiful eagle feathers. In return, Johnny gave them a mirror that his mother had brought west with her. Although the Indians had often seen the reflection of their faces in streams and ponds, they had never before seen a mirror. They laughed as they made funny faces in the mirror.

Mrs. Tyler noticed that the Indians were paying a lot of attention to the calico shirt Mr. Tyler was wearing. Before I knew it she had traded the Indians two calico shirts for fish and vegetables.

RORY ran in circles barking. He was having a wonderful time — especially since the new friends were petting him and letting him lick their hands.

I have to admit that I got a little jealous. No one was paying any attention to me.

Each night my family built a fire.  Because wood was scarce, they often used buffalo chips which Johnny had gathered during the day.
The fire kept them all warm and
allowed Mrs. Tyler to  cook the evening meal.
It was very difficult for Mrs. Tyler
because she had to cook the entire meal bent over
which was very hard on her back.

She also had to be very careful that the prairie winds
didn't blow her long skirt into the fire.

The Tylers had brought Jesse from
home to provide milk

and chickens from home
provided eggs.

The eggs were often stored in the
bags of flour to keep them from
breaking during travel.

After dinner, dishes had to be washed.
When clean water was available, washing dishes was
not a big problem for Mrs. Tyler. She always had
trouble, though, figuring out where to set the dishes to drain.

Do you have any ideas that
would have been of help to her?

(This was my idea but then, what does an ox know about washing dishes?)

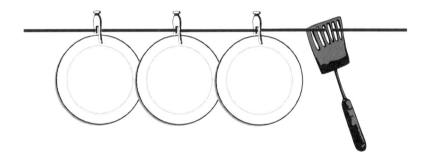

Each night Mrs. Tyler said goodnight to Johnny and gave
him a kiss. But before she could go to sleep,
she had to see to the mending and get things
ready for an early breakfast. She was very,
very tired by the time she got
to lay her head down on a pillow.

Do you know what a butter churn looks like?
Here's a picture of one in case you don't.

Women used to put milk in the churn and pump the
handle up and down until the cream rose to the top and
became butter. It was a very time consuming and
tiresome job.

Mrs. Tyler was very smart and very clever. Sometimes, when she wanted to have biscuits and butter for the evening meal, she got up very early to milk our cow, Jesse.

Then she put Jesse's milk in the butter churn and put the butter churn in the back of the wagon.

Now that old churn would bounce and shake over the rough trail all day so that by the time we set up camp for the night, all the extra cream had already turned to butter.

This was RORY's favorite part of the trip because he could roll over on his back and slurp up all the milk that spilled during the day as fast as it spilled. It made him so happy people two wagons away could hear his tail thumping.

Johnny worried, though. And he worried a lot more than he let anyone know. He worried about everything. Would the food hold out? Would they make it to Oregon before the snows came? Were there Indians up ahead who were not as friendly as the ones they had encountered earlier in the trip?

He also worried that his mother and father were getting too thin. (He knew that they often went without food to make sure there was enough for him.) He worried that RORY was getting weak. He worried because his mom looked so tired and rarely smiled anymore. He worried because his father looked so much older than when they began the journey. He worried because their clothes were becoming very worn and the canvas covering the wagon had been torn to shreds by wind and weather. He worried that maybe there was no Oregon and that all the traveling was leading nowhere. He worried and worried, and when he worried about these things, he talked to his best friend in the whole world, - and that helped a lot.

And sometimes at night, Johnny got scared.

You see,
when the
weather
was good,
Johnny slept
under the
wagon
and
often he
heard things.

In his mind, he knew he was hearing the hoot, hoot
of an owl or the howl of a coyote.

His mind told him all was okay,
but Johnny still got scared.  (Even though I was a
very big, strong ox, I sometimes got scared too.)

RORY stayed close to Johnny to reassure him that
he would always be there to protect him.

Sometimes when Johnny couldn't sleep, but he didn't want
anyone to know he was afraid, he would lay on his back
and look up at the sky.
It was SO-O-O-O-O big and seemed
to go on forever and ever.
Often, he made wishes on the stars.

Do you ever wish on stars?
I, Ollie, being the ox pulling the wagon, just wished we would
hurry up and get to this place called *Oregon!*

Each morning at daybreak we started out again.
It was important to get as many miles behind us
each day as possible.

We had to reach Oregon before we were stopped by
winter snows which could trap us in the mountains.
We knew that if that happened,
we wouldn't survive.

So we kept going.

Finally, we reached Oregon, but our struggle wasn't over yet.
Herb and I believe the last 14 miles around Mt. Hood, a huge

mountain in Oregon, were the worst part of the entire trip. The trail was steep and rocky. We had to make our way through huge mud holes and we had to stop to move many fallen trees.

I was so tired that I was ready to give up.

But finally, after months of traveling, and just
when we thought we could go no farther,
we made it!

We made it all the
way to the end of the
Oregon Trail and were
finally looking at the
land on which we
would make
our new home.

HIP HIP
HOORAY!

*HOORAY!!!
WE MADE
IT!!!!!*

YEAH! WOW!
I CAN'T BELIEVE WE
DID IT!!

Johnny **CHEERED** until his throat was sore.
He **CHEERED** and he **CHEERED** and he **CHEERED!**

And **RORY** couldn't stop
barking for joy!

BARK, BARK, BARK, WOOF, WOOF,
BARK, BARK, WOOF, BARK, WOOF,
WOOF, WOOF, BARK, HOWL, HOWL,
BARK, BARK, WOOF, HOWL, WOOF,
BARK, BARK, BARK, WOOF, HOWL,
WOOF, WOOF, WOOF, BARK!

Even Herb smiled, although he
turned his face away so that no one
would see.

And thanks to ME, OLLIE OX

..........oh, and I guess,
grumpy old Herb.........

everyone was safe.

Everyone was also very tired.

I wanted to sleep for at least a month, but I found
out my family still needed my help.

After a short rest, I had to help provide my family
with shelter and safety.  They needed a house in
which to live, eat and sleep.
And they needed it before winter!
So Mr. Tyler, Herb and I went to work.
(You can just imagine how happy Herb was to find
out there was even more expected
of him!!)

He was really upset!!  He made
terrible sounds I never knew an
ox could make!

First, trees had to be cut down.  Each time one fell,
*"TIMBER"*
was yelled to warn everyone
to get out of the way.

My Tyler was really, really loud when he yelled!
Johnny's *"TIMBER"* was almost as loud as his
father's, but not quite.

(How is your *"TIMBER"*?!)

Herb and I had to drag logs over near the creek where the house was to be built.

(Do you know what this is?)

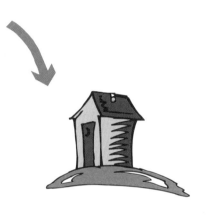

The house had to be near the creek so that carrying buckets of water to the house wouldn't be too difficult.

If the Tylers wanted hot water, they had to heat the water they carried from the creek over a fire. The good part for Johnny was that he didn't have to take too many baths because it was so much work to carry and heat the water.

Sometimes it was just easier and a lot more fun to jump in the creek to get clean.

We then built a shelter behind the house that would keep
Herb and me safe and warm
during the winter cold.

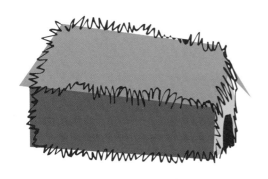

Now Herb and I would get a
chance to rest – at least until
Spring.  Then the fields would
have to be cleared and plowed so that the seeds we
brought from Missouri could be sown.  That was
going to be another big job that would
take a lot of strength.

I don't think we should tell Herb
about that until after he has a long,
long nap.  Maybe then he will be able to handle the
news without getting too grouchy.
I doubt it, though.

I was proud of what I had accomplished, and, although I knew he would never admit it, Herb was proud too. We had gotten our family, the Tylers, safely through their incredible journey and we had played a major role in building them a new home.

YES, I, OLLIE, FELT VERY PROUD.
AFTER ALL, WHO WOULD HAVE THOUGHT AN
OX FROM SUCH HUMBLE BEGINNINGS WOULD
GO ON TO PLAY A MAJOR
ROLE IN SETTLING THE
WEST AND CREATING THIS
GREAT COUNTRY

So the next time you are in the car with your family and you want to ask, "How much farther?" or "How long 'til we get there?", think of Ollie having to walk all the way across the country.

(Or for the Tylers -
A New Beginning)